Laurie Lunsford, author and illustrator, is a mom to three grown sons, and she is also a grandma. This is her 6th children's book. She is a retired elementary school art teacher. Now, she spends her days with people of all ages interacting socially through art. Art, as a healing agent, brings healing to the many lives that have been touched through art.

This book is dedicated to Logan Lunsford

Logan's Shadow

by Laurie Lunsford

On a snowy day

Logan discovered her shadow

She moved and the shadow moved

Her shadow looked tall in the snow

As the sun went down

Day after day

She found many things

To do with her shadow

On the wall

Logan's shape moves

She flaps her arms

Like the wings of a bird

And the bird flies

And she thinks about spring

And the birds singing in the trees

On the wall

Logan's shape moves

She raises her arms

To make them pointed

And her rocket shadow gets ready for take-off

And she thinks about going up in a rocket

Above the clouds

On the wall

Logan sees her shadow

Her dog jumps up

To give her a kiss

And her camel shadow raises his head

And she thinks about a camel in sunglasses

Walking across the hot desert

On the floor

Logan sees her shadow

She moves one leg in the air

Then she moves it back down

Her alligator shadow opens and closes his mouth

And she thinks about an alligator that talks

On the sidewalk

Logan's shadow moves

She makes claws like a bear

And moves them up and down

And her bear shadow waves his claws

And she thinks about a friendly bear

walking through the woods

In the grass

Logan's shadow moves

She makes her body stretch

And wiggles it back and forth

And her snake shadow slithers

And she thinks about a snake

As he discovers what is living

Down in the grass

On the big tree

Logan's shadow moves

She spreads her arms

Straight out

And her shadow hugs the tree

And she thinks about someone who loves her

It is night time

There is no shape that moves

There is no light

Logan goes to sleep

And dreams about an alligator talking to a bear

And about hugs

From those who love her

Made in United States
Orlando, FL
30 November 2024

54382404R10022